MUM
GOT SICK

TINA MITCHELL

AuthorHouse™ UK
1663 Liberty Drive
Bloomington, IN 47403 USA
www.authorhouse.co.uk
Phone: UK TFN: 0800 0148641 (Toll Free inside the UK)
        UK Local: (02) 0369 56322 (+44 20 3695 6322 from outside the UK)

Published by AuthorHouse 12/18/2021

ISBN: 978-1-6655-9566-7 (sc)
ISBN: 978-1-6655-9567-4 (hc)
ISBN: 978-1-6655-9568-1 (e)

DEDICATION

Tina Mitchell grew up on a council estate with her parents and younger sister Cherie. Tina was a rebellious child at school and left with no qualifications. Unfortunately Cherie died of cancer aged 45, Tina was absolutely devastated from this. Life has thrown many challenges at Tina but this has been her hardest one yet. This book is not about Cherie's story of cancer it could be someone else's journey.

Cherie you will always be my hero.

1

Mum was sick.

Mum was shouting again. "Come on, Lucy. We are going to be late for the nurse." Mum was having another blood test. She said the nurse wanted some of her body petrol because she was always feeling sleepy. When we got to the doctors, the nurse was running late, which Mum wasn't really happy about. The nurse took some of Mum's blood and put a plaster on her arm. I got a sticker for watching.

Let me introduce myself. My name is Lucy, and I am eleven years old. I live in a big house with my mum and dad. I don't have any brothers or sisters, but I do have a rabbit. She's called Jumper and lives indoor with us. She can do tricks when I ring a bell.

It was summer holidays. The sun was shining, so the paddling pool was up. My mum doesn't work, so she was at home. I don't have to go to any holiday clubs or to a child minder, not like some of my friends who hardly ever see their mums or dads. My dad works in London, and he gets loads of money for his job. That's all I know.

When we got back from the doctors, Mum and I put the hose pipe into the paddling pool. Why did it seem to take forever to fill up? While the paddling pool was filling, I went indoors and brought out Jumper so she could play in the garden and get some fresh air. When the pool was ready, I jumped straight in, and it's was absolutely bloody freezing! Mum told me off for swearing.

I'm planned to stay in the pool all day, until I got all wrinkly. Mum sat on a sun lounger, and after a while, she fell asleep. I hoped all summer would be like this because this year we aren't going on a seaside holiday. That's so not fair.

Mum woken up just before Dad came home from work. I was still in the paddling pool, and Jumper was hopping around the garden. Dad asked if we wanted a cold drink. He brought me out a glass of squash, Mum had a glass of wine, and Dad had a beer. After she finished her wine, Mum started dinner. Another salad again with potatoes. This is the only thing I did not like about summer—salads every day. We ate what Jumper ate.

Once dinner was ready, Mum called me and Dad in to wash our hands and sit at the table for dinner. At the dinner table we told each other about our days. I told Dad I got a sticker from the nurse because I was good at watching Mum having a blood test. Mum told Dad all about her blood test and how she was feeling. She said the results would be back within a few days.

During the summer it doesn't get dark till late. But I still have to go to bed at 8.30 p.m. That's not fair when it's the summer holidays. I'm only allowed to stay up late on Saturday night, and that's until 9.30. I can't wait to be a grown-up, stay up really late, and eat and do what I want. It's not much fun being eleven years old.

Over the next few days, Mum and I did nothing. We just stayed at home and spent a lot of time in the garden. I'm glad the sun was hot and shining. I was in the paddling pool all day, Mum lay on the sun lounger, falling asleep. And poor Dad was at work.

On Wednesday, Mum got a call on her mobile phone from the doctors' surgery, asking if she could come in and have another blood test because her white blood cell count was low. I didn't understand that because Mum always called it body petrol as the blood in your body has to go all the way round to your heart, lungs, brain—everywhere. Mum say's it's just like a car that needs petrol to make it go. Our blood makes us go. Mum made an appointment for the next day.

Thursday we were back there at Mum's doctor. This time the doctor took Mum's blood and then her blood pressure. The

3

doctor asked lots of questions. I just sat on a chair, swinging my legs and looking at a big poster of the human skeleton. We have loads of bones in our bodies. Imagine if we had no bones our body. We would be just like jelly on the floor.

I was daydreaming so I didn't notice the doctor was talking to me. Mum had to shout at me. The doctor told me that I had to be good as Mummy was poorly. I told the doctor I'm always good.

After the doctor's we went shopping. I hate shopping unless I'm getting toys or a Build-a-Bear for me. But this time it was only a little shop, and Mum only got a basket. She bought us doughnuts for after dinner. I couldn't wait for dinnertime, but I figured it would be salad again. I am so not a rabbit.

When we got home, Mum said it was too late to go in the paddling pool. She was just about to start dinner, and Dad would be home soon. Tonight we were having pasta for dinner. Hooray! I love pasta, and there would be no salad at all. And after dinner, a doughnut of course. Dinner was nearly ready when Dad came home. I set the table as I was being good, just as the doctor asked me to.

Mum was in the kitchen when Dad came home. He gave me a kiss, and then he went over to Mum and gave her a kiss as well. Dad said to Mum, "You don't look too well today. You look tired and a bit washed out."

Mum replied, "I don't feel too good today. Maybe it's because they took lots of blood. So after dinner I'm going to have a bath, go to bed early, and read a book."

I helped Dad clean up after dinner. Mum went upstairs to have a hot bubble bath. After her bath, Mum went to bed. It was really early because the sun was still shining. I wasn't going to bed yet; it wasn't my bedtime. Dad went upstairs to check on Mum. While he was up there, he changed out of his work clothes and into his home clothes.

When Dad came downstairs, he asked if I would like to go on a bike ride, and I said yes. Out came the helmets and bikes and off we went. We rode for miles up and down the hills and through the woods. It seemed we were out for hours. Finally Dad said, "It's time to make our way back now to check on Mum." Dad was right. I was tired, but I didn't want to tell him.

When we got home, it was 7.30, and Mum was fast asleep in bed. She must have been tired or really was very poorly. I only had a hour left before my bedtime, and I had to have a shower. It's so unfair at times. Well at least I got to spend time with Dad. Some of my friends at school didn't even have a dad.

After my shower I got my PJs on and got into bed and read for a little while. My legs were aching because of the bike ride.

Dad woke me the next morning as Mum was not feeling well. He took the day off work to look after Mum. Dad was taking me to Granny's. I got dressed and went into Mum and Dad's bedroom to say good morning to Mum. Mum looked really sad. She didn't have her usual happy face.

Dad called me down for breakfast. After breakfast, me and Dad went off to Granny's. When we arrived, she was waiting for me at the front door. *Something is not right,* I thought. But it was only a fleeting thought and then forgotten. Dad didn't even come in. As soon as I jumped out of the car, he was gone.

Mum and Dad picked me up from Granny's I couldn't remember the last time they both picked me up. As a treat we were going to the ice-cream parlour I loved. When we arrived, I chose the table at the window so I could be nosy. And if Mum and Dad went on about something, at least I could look outside. We ordered our ice creams; I ordered the biggest one. Mum just had a milkshake, and Dad had a waffle. Mum asked me about what I done at Granny's house, and I said, "Nothing much. Just watched the telly and playing videos games."

The lady brought us out our ice creams, and mine was massive. Dad said, "I hope you are going to eat that all up."

"No problem. I'm going to." Mum drank her milkshake, and Dad tucked into his waffle.

Then Mum said, "I had a call from the doctor regarding my blood. The doctor has arranged for me to go to the hospital for an MRI of my body on Tuesday just to see what's going on."

I asked her what an MRI scan is, and Dad explained, "It's magnetic resonance imaging which uses powerful magnets and radio waves throughout the body so it can see everything in your body." I don't know why he said all that. He just had to say it's like a giant magnifying glass. Mum and Dad said they would be honest and tell me the truth about Mum and what's making her feel so poorly. I just said okay. I didn't really take much notice because my ice cream was melting. I managed to eat all my ice cream up, and so did Dad. But Mum hardly drank any of her milkshake. Dad paid the bill, and we went home.

I couldn't wait to get home and get in the paddling pool as it was still up. There was more grass in the pool than there was on the ground, if you know what I mean. We had only been home for an hour or so when Mum got a call from the doctor's surgery to say they had a cancellation appointment for an MRI scan for the next day, Saturday, if she wanted to take it. Mum said yes. She wanted to know what was making her feel so poorly. Mum's appointment was for 11.30 a.m., so Dad was taking her, and I had to stay with my granny again. I didn't mind because the thing about Granny's house was she always had sweets everywhere, and you can just take them without asking.

It was coming up to 6.30 p.m., and we hadn't had dinner. I know, we had ice cream, but that's not dinner. Mum was lying on the sofa. Dad asked, "Shall we have pizza tonight?" I couldn't believe this. First ice cream and now pizza. This was the best day ever.

When the pizza arrived, Mum said she wasn't hungry. She still looked sad and didn't have that funniest face about her. She just didn't seem to be my mum at the moment. But she was Mum, if you know what I mean. I helped Dad tidy up. He put some washing in the machine, so he could hang on the line in the morning. Time was getting on, and I was getting tired. So I went to bed early to watch a bit of TV and then fall sleep. I wanted to wake up before Mum and Dad on Saturday and bring them coffee in bed as a surprise. Hopefully that would make Mum happy. I didn't like seeing my mum like this. I knew she was trying to be as normal as she could be around me.

I must have been really tried as I went to sleep straight away. I woke up and the clock said 2.46 a.m. So I went into the bathroom and got some water. Mum and Dad were in their bedroom, and they had the bedside lamp on. I could see that Mum was crying. Dad was saying to her, "Everything is going to be okay. It might be nothing, but if it is cancer, we will deal with it. We have some good friends, and we have the family support as well."

MUM GOT SICK

Mum and Dad had told me they would be honest and tell me everything that was happening. Yet there they were, in bed and talking about cancer. I went back into my bedroom and tried to get back to sleep. Thank God tomorrow was Saturday, and I could have a lie in.

2

"Come on, Lucy. It's time to get up," Dad said. "Half the day's already gone." I looked at the clock: 10 a.m. Sometimes Dad did go on a bit too much.

I really wanted to wake up earlier to make them coffee in bed. Maybe tomorrow I would do it. I had to get dressed in a rush as I had to be dropped at Granny's. I didn't have any breakfast and had bed hair, but never mind. Mum seemed a bit happier today. She smiled and kept on kissing me, which was nice.

While Mum and Dad were at the hospital, Granny and I went shopping. Granny treated me in the shops in the town. After we finished our shopping, we went back home. Mum and Dad were already there. I couldn't wait to try on all my new clothes. They all fit. Mum said, "You look beautiful and all grown up."

I went upstairs and put my new clothes away. When I came downstairs, they were all in the kitchen drinking coffee and talking about Mum's scan. I had a glass of Coke as Granny told Mum her gossip. I asked Mum about the scan and what it was like. Mum answered, "I had to lie on this very skinny bed. Then they gave me some earplugs because the machine was very loud. It was a very tight fit, like being in a tunnel. It felt like I was in there for ages, but it was only twenty minutes."

Dad suggested we have a barbecue and asked Granny if she wanted to stay for dinner. Happily she said yes. Saturday night was really fun. Dad did the food well, burgers and sausages which were black outside and pink inside. After dinner we all played games in the garden. I went to bed that night later than normal, which was good. I could not remember the last time we all played games and laughed together.

When I woke up Sunday morning, I had a surprise. Granny had stayed the night in the spare bedroom! Dad and Granny were both making a cooked breakfast. Yummy. Mum had hers in bed, but she didn't eat much. Dad said Mum was tired after yesterday, so we were having a lazy day. I do like lazy days as I can pretty much get away with anything.

After Dad and Granny cleaned up after breakfast, Dad took Granny home, and I stayed with Mum. Mum was in bed, so I got into bed with her and started asking some questions. I asked why they kept on taking blood out of her because it was slowing her down, just like a car does when it has no petrol.

Mum replied, "They think that I might have a bug, and it's eating my blood. That's why I'm so sleepy. Your blood has lots of different vitamins that help all parts of your body."

"Why did they want to look inside your body for magnets?"

Mum laughed, but I didn't understand why. She explained, "The scan sends magnetic images to a screen where they can see what's going on in your body. They took pictures, but it will take a couple of weeks before I get the results."

Dad came home shortly after our conversation. We did absolutely nothing that Sunday. Mum stayed in bed; Dad watched football through his closed eyelids. I had a great time eating what I wanted out of the cupboards.

After a while, Mum woke up and called for my dad. I went upstairs to see what she wanted and told her Dad was asleep. Mum wanted a glass of cold water, and I said I would get it for her. But she said she would come downstairs, get a drink, and sit in the garden for a little while. So Mum came down the stairs very slowly and holding on to the handrail. Mum got her water, and we both went out to sit in the garden. It was still sunny, and there was a light breeze. I asked Mum if she wanted a blanket, and she said no.

Jumper was having a great time in the garden. She's only allowed in garden when the sun has gone down, and it's not too hot. Otherwise, it could kill her, and I would be devastated.

I've never had anything or anyone I know die. It must be really sad.

Dad finally woke up and asked what time it was. He asked me, "Why is your mum downstairs and out in the garden?" I explained, and he asked her not to stay out there too long in case she got a cold. The time was coming up to 7.30 p.m., and Dad asked me to bring Jumper in and that it was about time Mum came in as the sun was setting, and the wind was picking up.

Dad helped Mum out of the chair, and as she slowly walked towards the back patio doors, she fell and hit her head on the paving slab. Dad panicked because there was a lot of blood. "Stay with Mum," he told me and went to call 999 for an ambulance. Dad got a cold wet tea towel and put it on Mum's head. Dad then rang Granny, told her what happened, and asked her to come over in a taxi so she could look after me while he went with Mum to hospital. Granny is my mum's only daughter. I don't have a grandad. He just cleared off one day. Well that's what my mum and granny say, so that was what I had been told.

Granny arrived before the ambulance, and Dad and Mum were glad about that. Granny was going to stay at our house again as it made more sense. That meant I could stay up well late.

When the ambulance arrived, the attendants asked a lot of questions and putting sticky things on my mum. The said her blood pressure was low, and her oxygen levels were also a bit low. This meant that her blood—or body petrol—was finding it hard to get round to her body, especially to her heart. So they were going to take her into hospital to give her some oxygen to help with her breathing, and they looked at the bump on her head. I found all this body stuff interesting. I thought maybe one day I might become a nurse or a doctor. They do make a lot of money. Dad packed a bag for Mum—just some wash things, knickers, and nightdress—and off they went.

It was nearly coming up to nine o'clock. Granny ordered Chinese, and we watched, a film that was so funny; I love it. Me and Granny watched telly for a little while. I must have fallen asleep because Granny woke me up and said it was midnight. I asked Granny if I could sleep with her as I was upset about Mum. "Of course you can, darling." I must have fallen asleep as soon as I got in bed because I can't remember anything else except waking up in the morning.

It was Monday and still no school—#lovinglife—but we only have four and half weeks left of summer holiday. Then I start big, big school, secondary school. Mum's still hadn't gotten me any of the uniforms yet. The way it was going, I'd be getting mine from the lost property box at school.

Granny had woken up before me and was downstairs. She said that mum was still in hospital, and Dad was with her. Dad had taken two weeks off work to look after Mum and me. Granny told me, "They are doing some more tests on your mum today. She is in the best place. At least they can find out what's wrong with her."

Later that day Granny's mobile rang. It was Dad. Why is it that old people have computers and mobile phones but don't know how to use them? My granny had her computer just for games, bingo, and her dating websites. She used her phone to try and message her friends, social media, and emails but hardly uses it to ring you on it! I don't understand old people.

Dad must have asked if Granny would stay another night as they were keeping Mum in hospital. But he said that he would be home later. Granny replied, "No problem." When Granny got off the phone, she shouted, "Right, Lucy. Get dressed. We are going to get your school uniform."

OMG, this is real. I'm going to big school.

I got dressed. Granny said, "Make sure you have clean socks on as you will be trying on school shoes." When we were ready, we walked down the road to the bus stop; we didn't have to wait very long. I was so excited. I didn't even think about my mum. Was that wrong of me? Did that mean I didn't care because I was excited about getting my new school uniform.

I looked out the bus window and started to feel sad. A little tear appeared in my eyes. Granny said, "What's wrong, Lucy? You were so excited. What's happened?"

"I was just thinking about Mum. That's all."

"Your mum is in the best place. The hospital will find what's wrong with her, and hopefully make her all better. Then she will be back to herself again."

"Yes, you're right, Granny." Our stop was the next one, right in the middle of the high street. I was glad we were on that bus because it was so hot. When we got off the bus, it felt like getting off an aeroplane in a hot country. We went straight to the school uniform store. I'd never tried on so many clothes in all my life. Skirts long or too short. School ties, blazer. I got everything on the list.

The next place was to get school shoes, and that was where Granny and I fell out. I wanted these really nice black ones with just a little heel. Granny said no. In the end I sat down, and Granny chose the shoes she thought were acceptable for school. They were all like primary-school shoes. In the end I just picked a pair.

After all that, we got something to eat. I was well hungry, so we went to the Seven Seas fish bar and had cod and chips with a buttered roll. I was so stuffed, I thought I would go *pop*. Granny paid the bill and we walked to the bus stop. Granny must have spent a fortune on the school uniform. Hopefully when we get home Mum and Dad will be home, and I can give them a fashion show of my school uniform.

I rang the bell on the bus so the driver would stop, and me and Granny got off the bus. As we were walking up the road, I saw Dad's car on the drive. *Hopefully Mum is home as well,* I thought. Granny had a key to the house, so she opened the door. Yes, Mum was home. She was awake, lying on the sofa with a blanket over her. I was so excited to show Mum and Dad my uniform, so I went straight upstairs to my bedroom and started to put the uniform on. Well I managed to put the skirt, shirt, and blazer on, but I couldn't do the school tie. I came downstairs, walked into the front room, and Mum started crying. I asked her why she was crying, and she said, "My little girl is all grown up. She's not my baby anymore."

Dad did the tie and kept showing me how to tie it, but I still couldn't do it. After my little fashion show, I hung up my uniform and changed back into my other clothes. I went downstairs, and Dad got me a drink. I sat next to Mum on the sofa. Granny was sitting in the armchair. Once Dad had gotten everybody drinks, Dad sat in the other chair. Mum and Dad said they had to talk to us. *I wonder if my mum is pregnant, that's why she has been so sick.*

Dad explained, "The tests Mum has been having found out that Mum has cancer.

All I knew about cancer was that you die of it. I sat on the sofa saying nothing. But in my head, everything was going round and round. But I couldn't get my words out. Mum and Dad were talking to me, but I couldn't hear them. My head was just scrambled thinking about me. After a minute, Dad asked, "Lucy, are you listening? Have you heard what I said?"

"Yes I did. Mum, you've got cancer. So what does that mean for us and Mum? Mum, what happens now?"

"I start hoping to start my treatment soon. I am having chemotherapy every other week for five weeks. And I shall be taking lots of different medication at different times."

"Then will you go back to being my mum again?"

"Lucy, there's nothing more in this world I would not give or do to be your mum again. The one who used to laugh and play games with you, go shopping, and make cakes. But I can't answer that question at the moment."

Dad said, "I will be home more, and Granny will be helping out. And you can go and stay at her house."

Then I asked *that* question, that question I wanted to know the answer to but didn't. "Mum, are you going to die?"

Mum answered, "We all have to die one day, sweetheart. That, unfortunately, is a fact of life. When your body clock stops, and your lifelong batteries have run out, that's when you are called to heaven because your life's work on earth is done. But believe me, Lucy darling, I promise you that I will try my hardest to get well again."

Everyone was sad and didn't say much. Maybe it was because I was there, so I said, "I'm going upstairs to my bedroom."

Mum asked, "Are you okay, Lucy?"

"Yes I am." Then I went over, gave her a kiss, and then went to my bedroom.

Once in my room, I got my mobile phone and googled the word "cancer". It said that cancer occurs when cancerous cells grow in parts of the body and keep on growing and growing. They invade and destroy healthy cells and tissues in your body, including your organs. Then it came up with cancer as an astrological sign of the zodiac, and a constellation of stars which means a group of stars. *Oh,* I thought, *so when you do die of cancer, you become a star. That explains why there are so many stars in the sky at night.* Okay, that really confused me.

I was sure my mum would be okay as Mum and Dad said she would be getting chemotherapy. So I googled what chemotherapy was. It said it was an angry drug that quickly destroyed the growing cancer cells in the body. A doctor called an oncologist consultant would give her the treatments.

After reading all that information, it looked like Mum would be okay, so that put my mind at rest.

I went downstairs and told Mum, Dad, and Granny all that I had read. "There's nothing to worry," I said. "Cancer is a bad number of cells that turn cancerous and invade your healthy cells, so they are treated by chemotherapy—angry chemicals that try to kill the cancer. So Mum, after your five weeks of treatment, you will be all better. That will be great, Mum and Dad."

Mum and Dad just looked at each other with sad tearful eyes and then at me. Granny just said, "Let's hope and pray. Your mum is going to need lots of rest and quiet time, so we all have to pull together."

I continued, "And did you know that cancer is a zodiac star sign? And it's a group of stars called a constellation, so when a loved one does die of cancer, you can see that person at night as a bright shining star watching down on you. I bet you didn't know that."

Mum and Dad said at the same time, "No, Lucy, we didn't. But that's lovely to remember that."

I stayed downstairs for a little while, but it was only Granny talking about something that she was going to buy from China to help her aches and pains. But it would take months to arrive, and she would of forgotten about it by next week.

Granny asked if we were hungry. I answered, "No. We had a big lunch in town today." Mum and Dad said that they weren't hungry. It was probably the shock of the news Mum had today.

It wasn't late or dark at all, but I went up to my bedroom just to think about things. I hadn't even asked my mum where the cancer was or if her hair would fall out with the chemotherapy. I decided that in the morning, I would write a list of questions to ask Mum.

I didn't sleep very well that night, but I don't think anyone else did in the house. I went downstairs, and Granny was already up and had made my breakfast. I said, "Granny, I'm going to do a list of questions to ask Mum and Dad about her cancer. And if they don't have the answers, they can ask Mum's oncologist consultant for the answers. What do you think about that, Granny? Is that a good idea?"

"Yes, Lucy, it is."

3

After breakfast I went straight upstairs, got my best handwriting pen, and my book. Then I started to write down some questions.

1: How do you get cancer, and can other people catch it, like a cold?

2: Mum, where is your cancer in your body? And what does terminal but not curable mean?

3: Are you going to lose your beautiful brown hair from the chemotherapy?

4: Are you going to be sleepy and moody?

5: Will you have to stay in hospital?

6: Are you going to be sad all the time?

7: Are you going to be honest and tell me the truth?

8: And *if* you are going to die, please, can we all talk about it and what happens when you die?

9: Can I have a puppy, please?

Once I finished my list of questions, I got dressed, made my bed, opened my curtains and window, and went downstairs.

Dad was up, but Mum was still asleep in bed. I showed Dad and Granny my list of questions, and they said some of them were very important. But they had a little laugh, especially at the question number 9. Dad said, "What we will do is ask Mum if she wants to go on a picnic, and we can talk about it and answer your questions honestly. What do you think about that, is that a great idea?"

Granny said, "I'll have to pop home for a little while to get some other clothing and stuff." Dad said he would drop her home, and she just had to ring when she wanted picking up. Dad suggested that I go with Granny. I wondered, *Am I ever going to get any time on my own with my mum?*

We left for Granny's. Dad was dropping us off first. Then he was going to the supermarket for picnic things. Dad said he would pick us up in an hour.

Granny rushed around like a mad old lady. She doesn't do that at our house; she has everyone running around after her. I supposed that would change soon, when Mum starts her chemotherapy on the eighth of August.

Dad was tooting the horn outside Granny's house. She checked to make sure everything was turned off, and we went home. Mum was up and looked lovely. She wore a pretty, yellow, summer dress; her beautiful brown hair was in a ponytail. Dad and Granny sorted out the picnic, and I fed Jumper. To be honest, I had been neglecting her a bit.

With the picnic all sorted, we got into the car, and off we went. I had my questions in my pocket, ready to ask. We went to the local park. It is beautiful with big lots of woods, a lake, and a picnic area. We sat down on the picnic tables because Granny said, "If I get down, I won't be able to get up again." Mum said she wouldn't either.

In the picnic we had sausage rolls, sandwiches, crisps, chocolate cake, and little cans of Coke. I went to get a cake first, but Granny said to have a sandwich first. Then Mum said, "Just let her have whatever she wants. It's all got to be eaten anyway." Once I finished my cakes, I got my pen and list of questions all ready.

Then I started by asking Mum, "How do you get cancer, and can other people catch it just like a cold?"

"Lucy, you can't catch cancer like you catch a cold or tummy bug. Our bodies are made of cells. In fact, your body has more than a hundred million, million cells. That's a lot of cells. Cancer starts with changes in one cell or a group of them."

Then, "Mum, where is the cancer in your body?"

Lucy "unfortunately, they don't know because they can't find the primary cancer. This means just one cancer that's making you unwell. But I do have cancer of unknown primary which is my body and organs. That's what the scan showed. I had a biopsy done to find out which type of cancer and treatment is best for me. The hospital said that it is terminal. That means it won't go away. They can treat the cancer, but I won't ever be cancer-free because it's incurable."

What is a biopsy is where they take a small sample of your tissue and test it to find out if it's cancerous and what treatment will hopefully work. Lucy, do you know that there are more than two hundred types of cancers, and each is diagnosed and treated in different ways? Lucy, sometimes the treatment you are given might not work. Everybody is different. But the consultant is doing the best he can for me.

"Mum, will you lose your beautiful brown hair from the chemotherapy?"

"Lucy, they say that I probably will lose my hair. But it will grow back. It's only hair. If you look at the word 'chemotherapy,' what other word can you see in it?"

I don't know, Mum. What word?"

"In the middle of the word 'chemotherapy' is 'mother.' And what does a mother do? Lucy, everyone has had or has a mother. A mother tries to look after you when you are sick and poorly. This is what the chemotherapy hopefully will do for me—look after me and make me all better."

"Will it make you sleepy and moody?"

"Yes, I will be sleepy and moody. And Lucy, I will probably be sick sometimes. But I can't really answer that question because the chemotherapy affects everyone differently."

"Will you have to stay in hospital?"

"Oh, I hope not. I want to be in my own cosy bed, where you can join me sometimes for cuddles. And you can bring me breakfast in bed," Mum said with a smile.

"Mum, are you going to be sad all the time?"

"Lucy, I will be honest with you, I'm scared, and I don't want to be sick. I don't like feeling this way. And I don't like you seeing me this way. Lucy, you are my sunshine, and you always brighten up my day. So I will try not to be sad."

"Will you and Dad be honest with me and tell me the truth?"

"Lucy, your dad and I have been completely honest with you from the start. I know you are only 11 years old, but you are not a baby. Nor are you a grown-up yet. But bless you, it's hard at your age, especially as you are entering secondary school. You are not my baby anymore."

"Mum, I will always be your baby."

Then Dad asked, "What about me?" Mum laughed and just said that Dad was the biggest baby of all.

Getting back to my questions, I asked, "Mum, if you are going to die, can we all talk about it and what happens when you die?"

"Lucy, do you know what happens when you die?" I shook my head. "You know that I say we all have blood which goes round the body and I that it is our body's petrol. Then you have your body's life batteries, which are your body's organs, like your heart, lungs, brain, and everything in your body. As you know, Lucy, batteries don't last forever. And when your body's batteries run out, the sad thing is that unfortunately, you die. That's sad for everyone. When someone has died, everyone is really upset and cries. But sometimes people get really angry because the person died and left them. People have many emotions at this time.

"Lucy, if I do die, my body batteries will have stopped. But did you know everyone has a soul within their bodies? Did you know our lives are full of certificates from life to death, no matter how rich or famous you are? I have written a poem about certificates. Would you like to read it?"

"Yes please, Mum. I didn't know you wrote poetry."

"I'm full of surprises, Lucy."

I read:

The Certificates

The first certificate that you will receive in life is a birth certificate. This certificate is to prove who you are and a time to celebrate new beginnings.

The start of your life journey ahead.

The second certificate you may receive in life maybe a religious one from your baptism, to a christening, or even a name ceremony.

The third certificate you may receive is one of achievement for your education and the qualifications you have achieved throughout your time during school for your path on life's journey.

The fourth certificate you may receive in life is a marriage certificate, but not everyone will receive this one. To some, the idea of marriage is not of importance. Some people choose not to marry as they have been chosen to follow a vocation in life in a religious way.

And some people don't believe in marriage—full stop.

The fifth certificate you may receive is a birth certificate if you have been gifted with a child.

This is truly a blessing, and one to be treasured.

The sixth certificate you may receive could be divorce, the end or the start of something new.

The seventh certificate that you will receive, but not officially, is a death certificate.

The eighth certificate is the end to your life.

Your total existence, meaning everything, has stopped.

Your body's battery has ended, and your time is done.

Why is it that a certificate means achievement, a status of who and what you were and achieved?

Everything in life is on paper, from the start to the end.

So your loved ones receive your death certificate and start to arrange your funeral, which is a very sad time. When families make rash decisions and fall out with each other over money, material things, and the personal belongings of their loved one who has just passed.

This day is a celebration for them; it's not your day.

Your time will come.

Remember the first three letters of funeral

are

F, U, N,

so this is time to celebrate and remember them.

F: Fond memories to share and laugh about.

U: Unique and unforgettable memories to share.

N: Never forget to live; life is too short.

Don't feel guilty that your life is carrying on. In life there are a lot more certificates you can achieve than the ones listed above. But remember, in this world we are all the same, no matter what colour you are, what religion you believe in,

what sex you are, how rich or poor you are; we all will have them,

2 certificates

in common, and that's life and death.

"Lucy, your soul is made of memories that everyone can treasure. And although your body may have died, which is sad, you will always have memories. The sad thing about death is that your body has to be prepared for its next journey. This happens at a funeral. Your body is put into a box called a coffin. These can be wooden, cardboard, or even wicker. Family members make sure that you are dressed in their best or favourite clothes. They say that a coffin is a gift box because the most precious things are in beautiful boxes. Then at the celebration funeral, the coffin is placed into the ground of the garden of a church. Sometimes a service is held at a crematorium, and the coffin is then placed into a really hot fire called am incinerator. If you have had your celebration funeral at a crematorium, you will receive a small gift box with the ashes of your loved one.

"I know this all sounds shocking and upsetting because this is something that happened to someone you love. But unfortunately, you can't have a dead person still with you. And like all things that have died, they start to smell, other things happens, and it's not nice. Lucy, everyone dies. No matter how rich or famous you are, we all will die. Some people have different beliefs and religions regarding death and do things very differently, but they still end up the same way and go to heaven. By giving this gift, your body, at a funeral, then you are gifted in return with beautiful flowers, rainbows, butterflies, and all the beautiful things that are around you as a thank you. But what you have to remember is that although this is sad, the person who died has gifted you with memories, and that is priceless.

"Enough of that talk. Hopefully we won't have to have this conversation. But Lucy, if I am going to die, yes, I will tell you. And yes, we can talk about it. You can help me arrange my funeral. But remember the first three letters of funeral are F, U, N. So when the time comes, we will make my funeral fun and not sad."

"My last question is, can I have a puppy, please?"

"Lucy, don't push your luck asking for a puppy. Dad's going to have enough to do with looking after me. Maybe when I get better, we will talk about it again."

"That's so not fair. Did you known that "dog" spelt backwards is God and is a man, and a man's best friend is a dog."

"Lucy, I didn't know that. You certainly have educated as all today," Mum said with a laugh. "Thank you for today. I have really enjoyed my day with my family. Now we all have to try and be positive and enjoy the days ahead of us. We must make them count as I start my treatment on Tuesday."

We all helped to pack what food was left and headed home. On the way home Granny said, "Can you drop me off at my house? I think I shall stay there tonight so you can have some family time before the treatment starts on Tuesday."

Mum had to go to the hospital anyway for a blood test to check her white cells, red cells, and some platelets. I had never known how complicated the body was and what stupid names your body parts had. It's just crazy. Imagine remembering all this to become a doctor or even a consultant.

Sunday night me, Mum, and Dad just relaxed and talked about holidays that we have had and about Christmas. Hopefully by Christmas Mum would be back to normal again, and we could really celebrate.

Tuesday morning Dad went and picked up Granny. While he was gone, Mum called, "Lucy, can you come here please."

Mum was upstairs in her bedroom, so I ran up the stairs. "Yes, Mum, what's wrong?"

"Lucy, if you have any questions, just ask. I don't know how the chemotherapy will affect me. I've got tablets every day, and every other I shall be having my chemotherapy. They give you your chemotherapy through a drip, and they will have to put a cannula in my arm. That is a short thin tube that is put into my vein, so the chemotherapy drugs can get straight into my bloodstream. This takes about two to three hours of just sitting in a chair, looking at other cancer patients. So Lucy, you will have to help Dad and Granny by doing jobs around the house. And your first job today is cleaning out Jumper's cage. I won't be able to do this, so it's your job. I have to have plenty of rest. The more rest I have hopefully will help me get better sooner."

"I love you, Mum. Don't worry, we will all look after you."

Mum gave me a kiss. "Lucy, I love you very much, and you are extremely special to me."

Dad walked through the front door with Granny. The first thing Granny said was, "I'm starving. I haven't had my breakfast." She put the kettle on and asked who wanted a cup of tea. Dad and Mum said no.

Dad told Mum, "We best make a move." Mum looked sad. *I bet she is a bit scared. I would be.*

"Lucy, don't forget what I said, please."

"No, Mum, I won't." And they went out the front door.

Granny asked what Mum meant when she said, "Don't forget." Granny can be so nosy. "Mum said I have to clean out Jumper's cage and be responsible for her. And she said I have to help you and Dad."

Granny had a cup of tea and banana on toast. I had chocolate spread and banana on toast. It was yummy. After breakfast the first thing that me and Granny did was clean out Jumper's cage. We took Jumper out of the cage, and she jumped around the kitchen. Granny did most of the cleaning; I just sat and watched her. "Granny, I'm going to do some research, so Mum won't be so scared. What do you think?"

"Lucy, that's a great idea for your Mum and for all of us, so we know a bit more about cancer."

4

I turned on my computer on and started to research cancer. The first thing that I'm decided to research was how cancers start. I found out that all cancers begin with changes in a single cell or group of cells. All cells have a control centre called a nucleus. Inside the nucleus are chromosomes that make up thousands of different genes. These genes contain hundreds and thousands of strings of DNA. Everyone's DNA is different, and this is your body's story. Sometimes your DNA sends coded messages to other cells in your body, and that can make them misbehave. Sometimes cells can be faulty or even missing from your DNA. This can cause some serious health problems, like Mum's cancer. Sometimes the faulty cells can divide and multiply too much. They can form a lump called a tumour. A tumour where the cancer starts is called a primary tumour. Some cancers start from blood cells. Those don't form solid tumours.

Next I looked up why some people get cancer and others don't? It seemed that cancer doesn't choose who gets it and who doesn't. Babies, young children, grown-ups, and old people, even animals, can get cancer. They said one out of two people will get cancer. That's half your family and friends. No wonder there are lots of flowers, butterflies, and rainbows. I had never really thought about that.

Then I found something called 'cancer staging,' so I looked that up. This what they called it when they do tests to see how big the cancer is and if it spread to other parts of the body. According to my research, staging was really important because it helps doctors determine the best treatment plans. I read that cancers are graded in different stages based on how bad they are and the prognoses. Some cancers are not as bad as others, and you have a better chance of living. Cancer is also graded on how much the cancer has grown and spread, and this defined how long you have to live.

I looked on my computer for ages. Cancer was so complicated. You have to be a brain scientist to understand. The big words, different grades, and numbers made me wonder if they really knew a lot about cancer as there was really no cure. Some people had cancer and was cured only to find it came back years later, and they died. So it gets you in the end.

I looked up the side effects of the chemotherapy. It definitely didn't seem pleasant. But Mum only has five weeks of it, and once a week on a Tuesday. So her last one would be Tuesday, 5 September. And I start school on the seventh. So Mum would be here to see me in my uniform. Maybe Mum and Dad would drive me to school.

5

I was getting bored looking for cancer stuff, so I started playing with Jumper. I didn't think Granny had noticed that she's in my bedroom. I just had to make sure I cleaned up her poo. Thank God it's only little ones. Jumper is my best friend. I told her everything. Sometimes I dressed her in my teddy bears' clothes. She looked cute. She even has a lead so I can walk her. But I only took her round the garden. I tried to teach her tricks using a bell.

I decided to make an obstacle course for Jumper and do a show for Mum to cheer her up. I started to look in my bedroom to see if I could find anything to use for the course. I wanted something that she could jump over, a tunnel thing, and a see-saw. She already sat up on her own. I was so excited.

But I couldn't find anything in my bedroom, so I went outside. Granny asked what I was up to. When I said nothing, Granny said, "It doesn't look like nothing."

I went into the shed and found a green pop-up basket that mum used for the weeds. I thought, *I can cut out the bottom of it, and that's the tunnel. Mum can get another one at the pound shop.* Then I remembered I had a ramp when I went through my scooter phase, so I pulled and moved things out of the way. I found it, so all I needed was something Jumper could jump over.

As I'm looking in the shed, Granny started shouting. "I'm bloody busy," I said to myself. "Granny, what do you want?"

"Where's that rabbit?"

"Upstairs, in my bedroom."

"Get that animal down now. Rabbits do not live in bedrooms."

Granny can be a moaner sometimes. "I will go and get her and bring her out to the garden." So I went upstairs to my bedroom, but I couldn't find Jumper. She wasn't under the bed, so I looked everywhere. But I couldn't find her. There was lots of poo, but no rabbit. I went into Mum and Dad's room and checked everywhere. Still couldn't find her. Next I checked Granny's room, and still nothing.

The last place was the bathroom. I so hope she hadn't gone in the bathroom as Dad was in the middle of decorating and had moved the shower and bath to different places, so there were some floorboards up. I went into the bathroom, and what do you know? She has been in the bathroom because there's poo. And yes, she was under the floorboards. Granny was going to go absolutely mad. I went downstairs and said, "Granny, Jumper is in the bathroom under the floorboards."

"What? For God's sake, Lucy. What are we going to do? I'll get a carrot, and she will come out."

"Granny, she won't come out just for a carrot."

"What are we going to do then, Lucy know-it-all?"

"Jumper likes toast, so I shall make her some toast and get her bell."

"Toast?" granny said. "I've never heard anything so silly in my life."

"Yes, and it has to be brown bread."

"Is Jumper on a diet and watching her weight?"

"No, Granny. It's just better for her." I put two slices of brown bread in the toaster for Jumper. After a couple minutes, the toast popped up and Granny took it out. "Granny, that's not cooked enough for Jumper."

"Whatever," said Granny. She put the toast back in the toaster to toast a bit more. Then a few minutes later the toast popped up again, and Granny asked, "Is this better? Does Jumper want butter on her toast?"

"Oh Granny, you are so not funny." Why do old people think some things are funny, and they really are not? Must be their age.

Granny took the toast upstairs to the bathroom, and I went and got Jumper's bell. I'd been using this bell with Jumper for her obstacle course, but that's a secret. I went into the bathroom, and Granny was on her hands and knees, with her bum up in the air. It looked funny. "Lucy," she said, "can you help me? I'm stuck, I can't move."

I tried not to laugh. "How are you stuck, Granny?"

"My hand has gotten stuck under a pipe trying to get this rabbit. Have you got a torch?"

"No, but I will go and get my phone."

"Who are you going to ring, Lucy?"

"No one, Granny. It has a torch on it." I got my phone and gave it to Granny. She could see Jumper under the floorboards, just looking at her.

"Here, Jumper, come and get the toast."

"Granny, she's not a dog."

"What are we going to do?"

"Granny, I will get her." I put down some toast and rang the bell. She come jumping along to me.

Granny asked, "How do you do that?"

"I've been training her. Jumper will be doing a show for Mum to cheer her up."

Jumper was all dirty and had a cut on her foot. We cleaned her up, and Granny got some stuff to put on Jumper's foot. "Well that was eventful, wasn't it? Lucy, let's not say anything to Mum or Dad. They have had a hard emotional day, and this is really unimportant." She looked at the time. "It is nearly lunchtime, and we have done nothing this morning except catch your rabbit. Now put her in the cage and let Jumper rest. Lucy, what do you want for lunch, beans on toast?

"Yes Granny. Thank you."

Granny and I sat at the table, eating lunch. "Granny, how do you think Mum is getting on?"

"I don't know, Lucy. But Mum has taken some magazines, drinks, and snacks. She'll be okay. Your dad's with her. We need to make sure the house is all tidy because your mum can catch any germs. The chemotherapy it makes her immune system low, and she can catch anything and become very ill. And we don't want that."

"Okay. I will clean Jumper's cage. To make sure she doesn't run away, I shall put her in the pen."

Granny started on the downstairs toilet and then the kitchen. After I finished, I went into the front room and sorted the loads of cushions on the sofa. We didn't really use the front room. We spent most of our time in the kitchen as it has a sofa in there, and the doors open right into the garden. Me and Granny tidied up for about an hour and then had a rest. Granny had tea, and I had squash.

As we had tea, Mum and Dad came through the front door. What a surprise! And Mum looked normal. "Mum, Dad," I shouted, "you're home!"

"Calm down, Lucy. We have only been gone a few hours."

"Mum, you look normal. Are you all cured now?"

"I wish I was, Lucy, but unfortunately I'm not. But I'm really sleepy, so I might go to bed for an hour."

"Okay, Mum. No worries. I will be as quiet as a mouse."

"Okay, Lucy, thank you."

Granny asked Dad, "Well how did it go?"

"Lots of blood taking, different drips, and a lot of just sitting around. We were in a ward of about eight, so there were four chairs on one side and four on the other. You just sit there looking at each other. Just questions in your head asking what cancer they have. How old they are because chemotherapy just seems to make people look really old. How many sessions have they had? And really, is there any hope for any of them? It's just makes you think about your life and what you could be leaving behind. You get tired just sitting there. I could go to be by myself, but I'm going to spend some time with Lucy." Dad shouted, "Lucy, do you want to go on a bike ride?"

"Yes", I shouted back. We got the bikes ready, put our helmets on, and away we went. We had been riding for a little bit when Dad said, "Come on. Let's stop in this pub and get a drink." Dad had a beer, and I had a bottle of Coke with a cardboard straw. Dad started to talk to me about today and said that Mum was going to get very tired. "And sometimes she might get cross with you, Lucy, but she really doesn't mean to. Mummy loves you very much, and so do I. But these five weeks of treatment are going to be really tough as a family."

"Okay, Dad. I think I understand. I will try my double best to be good."

"I know you will, Lucy."

"Dad, are you scared for Mum?"

"Lucy, if I could take your mom's place and her pain and what she is going through, I would. Right. Come on, let's make a move back home. Maybe if we are lucky Granny will have sorted something out for dinner."

When we got home, Mum was downstairs in the kitchen. She looked wide awake and was very chatty with everyone. Mum suggested getting a takeaway tonight, and we all decided on Chinese. I love the big crisps we got from there. Dad ordered the Chinese, and I talked to Mum about the day and what happened. Mum said, "You spend a lot of time sitting down and looking at other people. The drips take ages to go down. The nurses are really nice. So next Monday I have to have a blood test and then go back for more chemotherapy on Tuesday. So now I have four weeks left, and they will go so quickly. The chemotherapy will all be finished. So hopefully, Lucy, I will be able to take you to big school for your first day, my big girl."

The doorbell rang, and it was dinner. I was starving hungry and couldn't wait. I grabbed the bag of the big crisps and had one. So did Jumper; she likes them as well. I put loads on my plate. "I hope you are going to eat all that up," Granny said.

"Yes, Granny, I will." If there were an eating race, my granny would win it hands down. She likes her food. Mum didn't put much on her plate, just some rice and noodles. Mum had to take so many tablets at all different times, if you turned her upside down, she would rattle. I felt sorry for my mum. I didn't like seeing her this way.

After dinner Mum was going to have a hot bath and an early night, so she would feel refreshed for tomorrow. The sky was still light, and I was practicing with Jumper and her jumps in the garden. Dad and Granny wanted to know what I was up to, but I told them it was a surprise.

Dad and Granny were talking about Mum. They thought I couldn't hear them, but I could hear every word. Dad said, "It was quite upsetting to see the other patients having chemotherapy. Some had hair, and some had lumps of hair missing. Their faces looking all bony. If I found it hard, how will Lucy cope with it all?"

"Let's just take each day as it comes," said Granny. "Nobody knows what's round the corner. We just have to be brave for everyone."

After listening to this, I put Jumper away and sat at the table. Granny got me a drink. "Dad, what shall we do tomorrow?" I asked.

Dad said he had to pop into the office for a few hours tomorrow morning and then had the rest of the afternoon free. "What would you like to do, Lucy?"

"Can we go crab fishing? We haven't done that for ages. And then have chips and ice cream?"

"Yes, why not, Lucy? Let's get some fresh sea air."

"Well I'm going to bed now. Good night, Granny. Good night, Dad." We had a group hug, and I kissed them both. "I love you, Granny. I love you, Dad. I will pop in to see if Mum is awake and say good night to her." The bedroom light was still on, so I went in. "Good night, Mum. I'm just going to bed. What you doing?"

Mum was sitting on her stool at her dressing table. "I'm just looking at my hair."

"Why?" I asked.

"Lucy, it's going to fall out, and that is making me sad."

"But Mum, you will still be pretty. And you still will be my mum. I love you." Mum started to cry. "I'm sorry Mum that I made you cry."

"I wish you didn't have to see me go through this, Lucy. This is only the first week. By weeks 2, 3, and 4, I will look completely different. And I will be weak, sleepy. I really don't know how I will be."

"You will be Mum, my mum."

"I love you, Lucy."

"I love you as well, Mum. Good night."

6

I was the last one to get out of bed Wednesday morning. When I went downstairs, Mum and Granny were in the kitchen. "Dad's at work," Mum said. "What do you want for breakfast, Lucy?"

"Can I have pancakes, please? Mum, did Dad tell you what we are doing when he gets home? We are going crab fishing and having chips and ice cream."

"Well Lucy, you better have your breakfast and get yourself ready."

"Okay, will do. Oh, Mum, how are you today? Are you feeling better?"

"Yes Lucy. I've had some breakfast and a cup of tea. Thank you for asking. Dad said we all have to be ready for 12.30, or he's not going. Okay?"

So I ran upstairs and put on my swimming costume, then a pair of shorts and a T-shirt. I quickly fed Jumper and then went into the shed to find the crab lines. Mum was wearing a pretty, pink, flowery dress. Granny wore gold and silver, and everything that was bling. The sun was going to bounce off her and blind people. Mum and Granny readied a bag of juice, water, and stuff we can pick at.

When Dad came in, I shouted, "We're ready."

"Give me five minutes, and then we will go."

I had the crab lines and some bacon. I love crab fishing. Once I caught a real fish on my crab line.

It only takes about forty-five minutes to get to the seaside from our house. The only thing that used to put Mum and Dad off going to the beach was trying to find a parking space, even with Granny's blue disability badge. "There's never enough space in these seaside places," Mum said.

When we eventually found a space, it was a mile walk. Well not really, but it seemed that way. Dad, Granny, and me took the bags, so Mum didn't have to carry anything. The weather was not too hot and not too cold. It was pleasant with a light breeze and a clear blue sky. While we were walking towards the beach, a seagull pooed on Granny's top. It was so funny. Well, me and Dad thought so. But Granny wasn't amused, and Mum just seemed to be in her own little world.

We got down to the beach, and it was really busy. Dad hired some deck chairs for Mum and Granny and me; Dad sat on a towel on the sand. "Why is it that the tide is always out?" I asked. Granny said it wouldn't be long before the sea was back in again.

We sat there for about half an hour, and I was getting bored. "Dad, can we go and get chips now? I'm hungry."

Granny said, "Yes, I'm hungry too." Granny's always hungry. Sometimes she says that it's me who wants ice cream or sweets, but it's really her. Me and dad went and got the chips. We weren't away for long.

When we got back, Mum was asleep in her deck chair, and Granny was on her phone. I gently woke Mum. "She said, "Them chips smell lovely." We had brought some paper plates from home, and we shared the chips. They had salt and vinegar on them already, so I tucked in straight away. Mum started to eat her chips. She had a mouth ulcer that seemed to appear just after her first chemotherapy, but she was using a mouthwash to help with them. Then Mum said, "These chips taste funny. They taste like dirty sweet potatoes. I'm sorry. I don't want these."

"Can I have yours then, Mum?" A little while after we had our chips we packed all our belongings and took them to the car. We went and got ice cream and sat on a bench, just watching the people. I loved wondering what was going on in people's lives and that nobody knew what was happening in my life.

Once we finished our ice cream, Mum asked if we could go home as she was getting tired. Together we all said, "No problem", and then laughed. As we headed home, I wondered, *Why is the journey home always quicker than going?*

When we got home, Mum laid on the sofa while Dad took Granny home for a few nights just to give us all a bit a space. Dad is lucky he can work from home, whatever his job is. When Dad got home he went into the office. Mum was still asleep. I got Jumper out of her cage, and we started to practice. I just knew Mum was going to love my show.

It seemed I was on my own in the garden for ages. Mum was asleep on the sofa, and Dad was in the office. I went in the office to see what he was up to. He was working at his laptop. There was a glass beside him. "What's that in that glass?" I asked.

"Whiskey. I'm just having a glass while I go through my emails and while your mum's asleep. Is Mum awake yet?"

"No, she's still sleeping."

"Okay, give me five more minutes, and I will sort out dinner for us all."

"Okay. I will put Jumper away and clear up my things in the garden."

Dad woke Mum up and asked her if she wanted anything to eat or drink. "I'm not really hungry, but I will have a ginger and lemon tea. I'm feeling a bit sleepy and sickly. I hope this passes."

Dad made Mum her drink and asked what I wanted for dinner. "Nuggets, waffles, and baked beans, please."

"Okay then. I shall have the same as you—kids' food. No posh food for me tonight." We both laughed. Dinner took twenty minutes, and while it was cooking, I sent the table. Mum really looked poorly. Dad had given her that ginger drink, and I got her some biscuits. My and Dad's dinner was ready, so I sat at the table. Dad joined me, and Mum rested on the sofa. Dad and I really enjoyed our dinner. He put the plates in the dishwasher. It was 7.30, and Mum was so tired she went to bed. Me and dad read the information leaflets they got from the hospital about Mum's cancer. Dad said, "These are a bit confusing. How can I explain them to you if I don't understand what the leaflets say. The only thing that makes sense is how poorly they will or could be. Nothing about explaining to teenagers."

I told him, "I can't be bothered looking at these anymore. I'm put the telly on."

"I'll join you," said Dad.

I got a text message from Gran, asking how everything was going. I told her everything was okay, we were not doing much, and Mum's in bed. She texted back, "Okay, love. I will see you tomorrow. Good night, sweetheart."

Dad poured himself another drink and flipping through the channels on the telly. He complained, "There's nothing on this telly. We have over four hundred channels, and I can't find anything to watch."

In the end I said, "I'm going to bed and watch my own telly. Night, Dad."

"Oh, you going to bed, Lucy?"

"Yes, Dad."

"Good night, darling. I love you dearly, Lucy, and don't forget that."

When I got upstairs, I put my head round Mum and Dad's bedroom door. She was fast asleep. I sat on the bed for a while and watched her sleep. She looked so beautiful. I gave her a kiss and said good night. I went into my bedroom. It was about 8.30 I put on my nightdress and got into bed. I had a few questions going round in my head what happens if my mum does died? Will my mum change and not be as much fun anymore? If my mum does die will dad or granny look after me? Well I'm sleepy so let's not worry.

Today Granny's went out with her friends, and Dad had a meeting at the office, so I was at home with Mum for most of the day. To be honest, I was a bit scared. Dad was in the kitchen doing breakfast. Mum just wanted toast without butter and her ginger and lemon tea. Dad said Mum was feeling poorly today and was staying in bed for the day.

"Dad, are you going to be at the office for long, just in case Mum takes really ill?

"Lucy, I will be two hours at the most, and Mum should still be in bed. If Mum's awake, get in bed with her. I'm sorry, Lucy, but I've got to sort out all my work I can do from home. Unfortunately we don't how Mum is going to react to her treatment and how long Mum is going to be poorly."

"Okay, Dad."

"Lucy, ring me if anything happens, okay?"

I went upstairs, and Mum was still asleep. I went into my bedroom and got dressed. Great. How boring it would be today. I hadn't seen any of my school friends. I have been alone all summer holiday. Some of my friends have so much freedom but I don't. And my friends take the piss out of me. I dress like an old-fashioned girl. Sometimes I think my mum is in a time warp with my clothes. The only trendy thing I have is a mobile phone. You can imagine what secondary school is going to be like for me with the bullying.

I have been getting text messages from my friend Kate. She's eleven years old, the same age as I am. She has a twin brother called Joe. Even though Kate was my best friend, I had never stayed at her house or met her Mum and Dad, so I didn't really know much about her or her brother. Kate messages me every day to see if I want to go swimming or to the shopping centre. I keep making up lies about what I'm doing, but really, I'm doing nothing at home. So today messaged Kate and told her all about my mum and what's been going on. I just had to tell someone, and she is my bestie Kate messaged me back and said, "That's so sad what you are going through."

"Lucy", Mum shouted.

"Yes, Mum. Coming."

I went into the bedroom, and Mum was sitting up. "What do you want to do today?" she asked.

"Nothing. Dad told me you have to stay in bed until he gets back from work."

"Well, Lucy, if I want to get up, I will get up. I will not have people dictate to me, whoever they are." Mum got dressed, went downstairs, and made some tea. She even had more toast.

"Mum, do you want me to do that."

"No, Lucy. I'm fine."

"Mum, how are you feeling with that radioactive stuff in your body? Do you glow in the dark?

"Lucy, you are hilarious. But I do have bright green wee. I'll be honest with you, I feel a bit sick but hungry today, so I don't know whether to eat something or not."

"Mum if I make you toast, it doesn't matter if you are sick. It will be all right. I will look after you."

By the time I made the tea and toast, Dad came home. "What are doing out of bed? You are meant to be resting."

"I'm okay. If I didn't feel okay, I would tell you, so stop keep telling me to rest."

"Dad, what are we doing today? My friend Kate texted me about going out to the park with her and some other friends. I've been in all summer holidays."

"Where and what time are you meeting her."

At the bus stop on Hasting's Road at 12.30. So I will need some money for bus fare."

"Lucy, I don't know about this. You are only 11."

"Please, can I go? I will have my phone with me."

"Okay, Lucy, you can go. And I'm trusting you."

"Thank you, Dad. I promise I will be good, and I won't let you down." So I texted Kate, saying I would meet her at the bus stop in Hastings Road.

Mum was sitting on the sofa in the kitchen room on her iPad. "Lucy, can you get my bag, please?" She opened her purse and gave me £10. "Don't tell Dad." I promised her I wouldn't. I couldn't believe it. I was allowed to meet my friends. Now I wondered what I would wear that was at least a bit fashionable. I would just have to wear leggings, my trainers, and a T-shirt.

As Dad was changing his work clothes, he reminded me, "Lucy, we are trusting you. Please don't let us down. We have enough going on at the moment."

"I won't, Dad. I promise." Dad gave me £10 and told me not to tell Mum. This was great, £20!

I was all ready. My phone was completely charged. I said goodbye to Mum, who was resting on the sofa. "Have a good time with your friends."

"I will, Mum. Will you be all right without me?"

"Of course I will."

Dad was putting some washing on. "Lucy, have a good time. Remember, please, to be responsible for your actions."

"Dad, I will be. What time do I have to be home at?"

"How about 6.30, just in time for dinner."

"Okay, I will.

"Have you got your phone? Lucy, you will need some money for bus fare and maybe a drink or something to eat. Here's £10. Be careful with it."

"Thank you. I will." I walked towards the front door. Both Mum and Dad shouted their goodbyes. "Bye," I shouted back and closed the door. OMG, £30 *from* Mum and Dad. This was great.

I walked towards Hastings Road to meet Kate at the bus stop. When I got to the bus stop, and Kate was there with her twin, Joe. Kate said that they were going into town. "Is that okay with you?"

"Yeah", I said. "I'm not fussy where we go. Are we meeting anyone else?"

Kate answered, "Yeah, we are meeting everyone at the gardens in the town. Most of them will be going to our new school." Kate is extremely confident, funny, and outgoing. And her clothes are really nice and suit her character. Joe was a bit of jack the lad, who just wants to fight everyone. He had some issues, but maybe that's just boys.

The bus pulled up at the bus stop, and we got on. The bus driver moaned at me because I gave him a £10 note. "You are taking all my change," he complained.

I apologised, and then Kate said, "Well next time you should bring more change then." I was so embarrassed. The bus ride was about ten minutes, and some of Kate's and Joe's friends got on the bus too. I was beginning to wonder if I had done the right thing by going out with Kate. Our stop was the next one. Joe stood up and was continuously pressed the bell to let the driver know we wanted to get off. The bus stopped, and we all jumped off and headed towards the gardens in the town. There was about fourteen or more people there of all ages. I thought, *Mum and Dad wouldn't be impressed with what I'm doing. But I can't say I'm going home because my mum and dad wouldn't want me to be hanging around with older kids who look like troublemakers.*

Kate asked me if I was okay. "Yeah, I'm okay. What are we going to be doing down here?" Kate asked me if I had any money for some alcohol. I told her, "I've got money but not for alcohol."

"Can you lend me some money?" Kate asked. "I will pay you back.

"I will lend you a tenner. That's all I've got." So I gave Kate the tenner. Once I gave Kate that money, she handed it to an older girl. It was a sunny day, so we sat on the grass, talking about going to secondary school, what it would be like, and how excited we were. Then, about ten minutes later, the older girl returned and gave Kate a carrier bag. "What's in the bag?" I asked. Kate told me it was a bottle of cider. I thought, *What a waste of money.*

Kate opened the bottle and started to drink it in the park. "Here you are, Lucy, have a drink. Go on. It's really nice."

I felt really pressured to have a drink. If I didn't, can you imagine the grief I would get at school. So I had a drink from the bottle. It was a bit disgusting to drink from the bottle after everyone else had. Kate and I had the bottle between us, and it was nearly gone. Kate had drank more than I had. I was feeling really good and silly. I think I was a little bit drunk? Kate asked if I had any more money. I said yes and gave her another tenner. Again she gave it to the older girl, who went and got us the cider. While we sat on the grass, someone was playing music which was different from what was played on the radio. I really didn't listen to music and the radio. Music was never on in our house.

The girl came back and handed the carrier bag over to Kate. It had another bottle of cider in it. "Go on, Lucy. Open the bottle and have a mouthful." So I did.

I must say I was enjoying myself. I had no worries about Mum and her illness, no Dad telling me to be quiet 'cause Mum's asleep, or even Granny saying something. With my friends I could be me, just Lucy.

"Lucy, are you having a good time?" Kate asked.

"Yes I am. Are you looking forward to secondary school and not being treated like a child?"

"Let's not talk about all that now. We have a few more weeks yet. I love this song. Do you want to dance?"

It was about 3 p.m., and I was drinking and dancing in the gardens in the middle of town. How bloody cool was I. Totally loving life. I was having a really good time drinking and dancing, not talking any notice of anyone. Then I got a text message from my dad telling me not to be late. I couldn't believe the time. It was now nearly 6 o'clock. I had £10 left, so I decided to get a taxi home. "Kate, I've got to get going I have to be home by 6.30. I've got this family thing going on tonight. It is going to be, well, boring. I would rather stay here, believe me."

"Okay, Lucy. I'll text you later. See you."

I walked towards the taxi rank to make it home for 6.30. The taxi ride was only about five minutes; it always took longer on the bus. I had the driver drop me off around the corner.

The taxi only cost £2.50. I gave the driver £10 and sat there waiting for my change. The taxi driver said, "Thank you very much."

I replied, "Can I have my change, please?"

"Oh, sorry. I thought that was a tip." The driver gave me my change, and I got out of the taxi. The time was 6.20. Yes, I was early. That was good for my first time being out. I just hoped they couldn't smell the cider. I wasn't drunk, but I was happy and in a very good mood.

I knocked on the door, and Dad answered. "Hello, Lucy. Well done! You are early, and I'm impressed. Did you have a good time? It looks like you did."

"Yeah, I did have a good time. And I met a lot of friends who will be at my new school. Is Mum awake?"

"No, she's asleep."

"Oh. Never mind. What have you been up to today, Dad?"

"Not much. Mum's been asleep most of the day."

"Do you think she will be like this over the next four weeks?"

"I think it's going to get worse, and Mum's going to be very poorly. But I'm glad you have had a good time. What do you want for dinner?"

"Dad, I'll do a sandwich later. I'm going to my bedroom for a while." As soon as I got into my bedroom I messaged Kate. She and Joe were on their way home. I thanked Kate and said I had a good time and we would have to do it again.

Kate said, "Maybe you can stay at my house before we go back to school."

"Yeah, that will be really good. Text you later, Lucy..xx."

I went downstairs. Dad was sitting on the sofa with his legs up and drinking whiskey. *I wonder if he has been drinking all day. I don't think Mum would be happy with that.* But I hadn't been an angel. "Dad, do you want a sandwich. I'm having a banana one and some crisps. Do you want anything?"

"No thank you. Come and sit and watch telly with me, and we can have a chat. I've not seen you all day. What you been up to today?"

"Just hanging out with Kate and her friends. Some of them will be at my new school."

"That's good, Lucy. Things won't be so bad then if you've made friends already. Your mum won't be so worried now."

"How has Mum been today?"

"She's been really sleepy and has a bit of a bad belly. But she has had some chicken soup. I think it's the tablets she is on that are making her poorly, put all them chemicals in her body."

"She won't have chemotherapy next week; it's every other week, so I suppose that's good for Mum. Dad, do you think this will change Mum?"

"What do you mean?"

"Well, this girl in my class, Nicola, said her mum died but then they brought her back to life. Nicola said that her mum wasn't her mum anymore, that she had really changed. She was scared to do anything just in case she would die."

"No, I don't think Mum will be anything like your friend's mum. What are your plans for tomorrow, Lucy?"

"I don't have anything planned, Dad."

"Then shall we do something? Granny will be over, and we can all go to the zoo."

"Why not! Let's do that.

"I will ring Granny, tell her our plans, and see if she wants to join us. But you know Granny. She will come because she's frightened of missing out." Dad rang Granny, who said she would love to come tomorrow.

I could hear Mum calling, so I ran upstairs. "Hello, Lucy. Have you had a good day today?"

"Yes, Mum, I have. I went out with Kate and her twin brother, Joe. They are the same age as me, and they both will be going to my new school. Some of Kate's friends I met today also go to our new school."

"It's nice that you will already know some people there."

"Dad said if you were feeling up to it we can go to the zoo tomorrow."

"That will be nice. I'm sure I will be feeling a lot better tomorrow. I'm just so sleepy."

"Do you want a drink or anything, Mum?"

"Yes, please. Lucy, can I have a cold lemonade and a small bowl of ice with strawberry sauce please."

"No problem, Mum. I think I shall join you and have the same."

I came downstairs, and Dad asked if Mum was okay. "Yes. Mum would like a glass of lemonade and a small bowl of ice with strawberry sauce."

"That sounds nice. I think I will have the same as well. Do you want some, Lucy?"

"Yes please."

"Okay. Go and keep your mum company, and I will bring it up to you both in bed." This was good—ice cream and lemonade in bed with my mum. Dad brought our lemonade and ice cream upstairs, and we talked about going to the zoo tomorrow. Dad said, "It's been years since I've been to a zoo."

After I finished my lemonade and ice cream, I went into my bedroom. I had left my phone upstairs on the charger, I had three missed calls from Kate and loads of text messages. I didn't ring or text Kate back. I just chilled in my room and then fell asleep.

7

Dad was the first one up the next morning and sorted out breakfast. Mum was lucky enough to have hers in bed. The tablets mum took in the morning and evening had to be taken with food, so Dad made her some toast, tea, and a piece of fruit. Mum was having a good day. She looked happy, and that was good. Dad shouted, "The sooner we are all ready, the sooner we can get gone."

Within forty-five minutes, we were all ready and on the way to collect Granny. The zoo was about an hour and half away. Mum kept getting hot turns, so one moment the air conditioning was on and then off and then on again. When we got to the zoo Dad parked in a disabled bay as granny has a blue badge. But to be honest, the walk from the car to the front of the zoo was miles away. At the main reception you could hire wheelchairs, so we asked if mum wanted one so it wouldn't be too much for her, and she agreed. I think Granny was well gutted that she couldn't get a chair and had to walk.

We walked around the zoo, poor Dad pushing Mum in the wheelchair up and down; it was very hilly and bumpy. But when we tried to find the animals, half of them weren't in there. After a few hours we got some lunch and drinks and sat down for a well-deserved rest. After lunch we went round the other half of the zoo. At the end of the zoo there was a little tea shop, so we all had a cup of tea and a piece of cake. Granny gave me some money for the gift shop, but it was just cuddly toys. But I did buy a postcard. I had decided that every place that I go with Mum I would buy a postcard and write a little note on the back of it. While Mum, Dad, and Granny were drinking their tea, I took the wheelchair back. Once our tea was all finished, we walked back to the car. Dad helped Mum into the car. On the way home mum fell asleep.

We had to stop at the supermarket, so I sat in the car with Mum, and Dad and Granny went in. They were in there for ages. And when they came out, they had a big trolley load. Mum was still asleep when Dad and Granny got back to the car. Granny put her shopping on one side of the car. Dad put our shopping on the other side. And mum was still asleep. We dropped Granny off. Over the next few days there were no plans, just to stay at home. Granny probably would be over or we would go to Granny's. Mum didn't have chemotherapy next week. She did have to have a blood test at the hospital, and that was about it. So hopefully I might be able to see Kate again.

Nothing much happened Friday and Saturday. Mum was sleeping a lot, and Granny came over. Dad was doing home jobs, but I also noticed that he was drinking a lot more whiskey. I wondered, *Shall I tell Granny? I best not. She's got enough on her plate with her daughter having cancer.* On Sunday Granny offered to make us dinner, so we went to her house. She fixed roast beef. It seemed like it had been ages since we had a roast dinner. The only thing is when you go to Granny's house for dinner, you have to wash the dishes as she doesn't have a dishwasher, and it's always me who has to wash the dishes. We stayed at Granny's for about five hours. Time went so quickly; normally it doesn't go that fast. It was coming up to six o'clock, and Mum wanted to go home as she was tired. But Mum was awake all day! Mum has a blood test at the hospital on Monday. Hopefully everything will be okay because all she has been doing is sleep. I could say that all I do is sleep, but mine is from boredom. It has felt like these summer holidays have gone so slowly. This was another early night for us.

Mum was taking a shower and washing her hair Monday morning. She noticed that some of her hair was falling. This upset her though they said it would happen. She didn't realise it would be so quick, although she has had one lot of chemotherapy via drip and the other in tablet form. When Mum came downstairs after her shower, she was still a bit upset. She sat at the dining table, and Dad kissed her on her forehead. I didn't like seeing my mum this way. It made me feel sad. Dad asked if Mum wanted tea, coffee, or toast. "No, just water please. Everything is tasting funny at the moment."

"Are you okay, Mum?"

"Yeah. I'm just a bit anxious, that's all."

Dad took Mum to the hospital, and I stayed home alone. While Mum and Dad were out, I practiced with Jumper for the show. Mum and Dad were only gone for about an hour. Some of the questions I had asked seemed to be coming true. I knew Mum was sick and tired, but it's a bit boring. All I have is my rabbit, and all she did was eat or poo. We still had weeks before we went back to school. There was going to be a long day and night ahead. Dad asked if I wanted to go to Granny's I said no because she would have me doing jobs, and I couldn't be bothered with that. I guessed I'd stay in my room.

Dad shouted up, "Do you want to go on a bike ride after dinner." It had only just gone past lunchtime. Dad was in his study working from home with a small glass of whiskey beside him. Mum would not be happy about it, but what could I say or do.

Dad started dinner early tonight as we were going on a bike ride. We were having curry and rice. Mum was just having chicken soup. While Dad was cooking, the telephone rang. It was the hospital regarding Mum's blood test results. They said her white blood cells were low, meaning she had an infection.

They also said that Mum's number of red blood cell count was also lower. This meant Mum had anaemia, which was why she so sleepy so often. Mum has to be at the hospital by 10.30 tomorrow morning for a blood transfusion. At least that explains why Mum has been so poorly.

Mum was up in bed when the hospital rang, so when Dad took up her soup, he told her what the hospital said. Mum asked if I wanted to go to Granny's tomorrow while she was in hospital. I asked, "Do I have to?"

"No. What about your friend Kate? Ring her, and see what she is up to tomorrow."

I messaged Kate and asked what she was doing tomorrow. I hoped she wouldn't take long to message me back. I hate waiting for a reply. I kept checking my phone to see if I had gotten a text message, but nothing. I decided to give it another half hour, and then I would ring Kate.

Mum didn't want any dinner after that phone call. Dad said, "Sorry, Lucy. We will have to go on a bike ride another day. I must ring Granny and tell her what's going on."

"No worries, Dad. I'm just going upstairs to see if Kate has texted."

And she had. "Hi, Lucy, not doing anything tomorrow, so I've asked my mum, and you can come over and stay if you want tomorrow night." I'd never been invited to a sleepover and really hoped I'd be allowed.

So I ran downstairs to ask Dad if I can stay at Kate's. He said yes! I messaged Kate back and asked her for her address so Dad could drop me off at her house in the morning, before they went to hospital about ten o'clock. Kate texted me straight back with her address. "Thanks," I sent back, "and see you tomorrow." OMG, I was so excited I couldn't wait. I started getting my bag ready for tomorrow.

Dad shouted upstairs, "What takeaway do you want?"

"Not hungry," I shouted back. Takeaway again. I'm so fed up with takeaway. That's all we have now. So Mum's in bed and not hungry, just tired, and Dad's downstairs drinking whiskey. And I had to look after myself. It seemed like our family was falling apart. If Granny knew what was going on, she wouldn't be happy. But I was lucky that Dad provided me with a takeaway most nights.

When Mum's awake, I was going to ask if I could borrow some of her make-up. But to be honest, if she said no, I was going to take it anyway. It's not as if she's going to wear it at the moment. So I settled on a plan. Mum and Dad have a walk-in wardrobe, so I hid in there until Mum was fast asleep. The tablets she took must really knock her right out. I grabbed her make-up and took just what I wanted and put it in a pencil case. I messaged Kate and told her that I was bringing my make-up with me. She messaged me back, "Can you get any drink?" to which I responded, "I'll see what I can do."

I went downstairs to see what Dad was up to, and he was asleep. So I went over to the sideboard, opened the doors, and found loads of alcohol. I don't know which one to take, so I took two—one bottle of vodka and a bottle of gin. I wrapped them in my PJs and put them in my bag. Then I decided to try and settle down for the night. It felt a bit like Christmas Eve, when you can't sleep because you are excited for Christmas Day.

Dad woke me at nine the next morning as he was dropping me off at Kate's house at ten. I had a quick shower and breakfast. When I came downstairs, Mum was up, but she looked grey, like she was made of concrete. She gave me a forced smile. I just went over to her and gave her a hug. "You'll be okay, Mum, once you have the new blood in you. You will be happy and back to yourself."

While I was talking to Mum, the telephone rang. It was Granny, and she wanted to speak to Mum. You know, it must be really hard and upsetting to see your daughter going through this, and as a mother, you can't physically help her. You can only be there for her emotionally. And it must be hard to put on a brave face when you are fearing the worst. Mum started crying when she was talking to Granny and saying things like, "Why me? Why have I got cancer? I can't take the pain no more. It's only been the first lot of chemotherapy, and I feel like this. I can't do it." I don't know what Granny said to her, but Mum's tears stopped. I know this sounds horrible, but I just wanted to get to Kate house. I couldn't wait. I was fed up with all this at my house.

Once Mum finished talking to Granny, we got our belongings together and got in the car. Kate house was only five minutes from ours. I was shocked to see her house. Not that I was posh, but it was a council house. On the drive was a car with no windscreen as it had been smashed. All four wheels were missing. It didn't even have a steering wheel. I couldn't believe it! All I knew about Kate was she had a twin brother, Joseph, and she was my best friend. I really think she's only my friend because I don't have any other friends. I think Mum and Dad were a bit shocked as well to see Kate's house, but they didn't stop me from staying there, which was good. "Goodbye, Lucy. Love you," Mum shouted out. I was so embarrassed.

Once my parents had gone. Kate said, "Come up to my bedroom."

We both ran up the stairs. Kate's mum shouted, "Can you stop running up them stairs? And don't slam your bedroom door." Well that was a bit too late as Kate had already slammed the door.

Kate told me that she hated her mum. "She is a bully towards me and Joe, and sometimes we are treated like slaves. We could be taken and put in care."

"You don't mean that, Kate."

"Believe me, Lucy, you haven't a clue what my life is like. We sat down on the bedroom floor. I didn't think the carpet had ever seen a hoover. I empty my bag. "Wow. I love your PJs, Lucy. They are cool." My PJs were only a silky top and short set in a baby pink.

"I'll leave them for you. You can have them."

"Really? You're not lying to me?"

"No. Why would I lie to you?"

"My mum lies to me all the time, and if I question her about a promise, she hits me. That's why I asked."

I gave Kate a cuddle and said, "I'm your friend. I wouldn't do that, and I'm sorry about what you go through in your home life. My home life is just as bad."

"Why?" asked Kate.

"My mum's got cancer. She's been having chemotherapy every other week. She had a test done, and she now needs a blood transfusion."

"OMG, Lucy. That's not good."

"I know. Everything has changed so much in our house. Now it's all about my mum, and I'm jealous of the attention she is getting. It used to be all about me, but now no one has time for me or my dad. My dad is constantly drinking while working from home. I think he's going to turn into an alcoholic with the amount he's been drinking lately."

"Sometimes I have a small drink as well, if it helps with sleeping and makes you forget all about what's going," Kate admitted. "Well what are we up to today? So have you brought some drink with you?"

"Of course."

"This is going to be amazing. Did you bring some money with you?"

"Yeah, I have some. Maybe we can get pizza. but I'm choosing 'cause I'm paying. What's your mum going to be up to today? Is she going to be in or popping out to the shops?"

"She will be going out later tonight and stay out all night."

"What do you mean 'all night'?"

"She will hang around some streets and then decide whose house she's going to stay in."

"Does she do this often?"

"All the time. We are always home alone. Parents are meant to be responsible and caring. I think they are just selfish. Shall we get ready and go out and get breakfast? We have no food in the cupboards. Shall I give Joe a shout as well?"

"Yes. We can go and get a bacon roll somewhere." Just before we left, I put my bag in Kate's bedroom. Dad had given me £30. I only took out £10, leaving two *£10 notes* in my bag. Also the bottles of vodka and gin were wrapped in my PJs. They weren't full bottles but only had a little drop taken out of them. We went out about 11 a.m. Kate and Joe's mum was still in the house. She wasn't very welcoming. She didn't talk much, and she didn't even look very clean. Even when my mum wasn't feeling her best, she always looked and smelt clean, nothing like Kate and Joe's mum. My mum worn bright, colourful clothes. Kate and Joe's mum was wearing stained black leggings and a dark purple top which was too big for her.

We went and got bacon rolls, and while we were there, we met up with some of Kate's and Joe's friends. They lived on a big estate, so everybody knew everyone. Kate and Joe told their friends that they were having a party tonight but to keep it quiet as they didn't want their mum there. The three of us spent the rest of the day just hanging out with Kate's and Joe's friends. It was great, and I loved it. The only company I spent time with were Mum, Dad, and Granny. Oh, and Jumper, which reminded me I must clean and feed her when I got home. I have really neglected her. Well, never mind. Can't do anything about that now.

It was coming up to 6 o'clock and we got a bag of chips to share as we walked back to Kate and Joe's house. When we got to the house, their mum was still home. She was so drunk she could hardly stand. And as for talking, she was just spitted some sorts of words out of her mouth. Katie and Joseph were so embarrassed, but I said not to worry about it. I went upstairs to Kate's bedroom to check that the vodka and gin were still in my bag. Both bottles were gone, along with the £20. What could I say to Kate and Joe? How could I say that she took them, that their mum is a thief and a drunk?

Kate came upstairs and asked me if I was okay. I said not really and told her what happened. Kate was absolutely furious with her mum. Kate said, "Don't tell Joe or it will all kick off."

We went downstairs, and Kate's mum said, "I'm going out now. Be good kids." She laughed and walked out the door.

I had texted my dad to see how Mum was, and he said she was sleeping. He asked if I was okay, and I said I wanted to come home and asked if he would pick me up. "No problem. Will be there in half an hour," he texted back. I don't think Kate and Joe were happy that I was going home, but I had the right hump. And to be honest, I just wanted to go home.

Dad pulled up outside the house and tooted. I thanked Kate and Joe for the day and told them I would see them soon. I jumped into the car. Dad asked, "Are you okay?"

"Yes. I just wanted to come home."

When I got home, Mum was awake. I asked how the blood transfusion went, and she said well, but it was boring just sitting there for hours. Dad made me and Mum hot chocolates with whipped cream and marshmallows. It was really nice.

After the hot chocolate, I went downstairs to see Jumper. I had not been looking after her, and that was very irresponsible of me as she is my pet. When I looked into the cage, she was asleep. I opened the cage so I could hold her. When I got her out of the cage, she seemed limp and floppy. She opened her eyes but didn't look well at all. I called for Dad, saying, "Jumper is not well." Dad came straight downstairs. "What do you expect? You haven't been looking after her."

"Do you think she will be okay?"

"Yes, I'm sure she will be. We will see how she is in the morning."

I didn't sleep very well that night because I kept thinking about Jumper. What would I do if she died? I told her everything, but I didn't even get to tell her about what happened at Kate's house. I woke up with the sunshine and the heat. My summer holidays are nearly over now, but so much had happened during this summer holidays, and I felt I had to grow up this summer. When I got downstairs, I could see that Jumper was still asleep in the cage. She was not sitting up, waiting to get out. I opened the cage door and stroked Jumper. She was breathing but had no energy. I started to cry. It was my fault. I didn't look after her properly. I neglected her. Dad came downstairs and started to make Mum's breakfast. He said he would ring the vet to get appointment for Jumper. After breakfast Dad rang the vet and got appointment for 11 a.m.

I got dressed, but my face and eyes were so red from crying. I went to see Mum. She asked if I wanted her to come with us, and I said, "Yes, please." Today mum was wearing a head scarf which was very pretty on her, and I told her that. Mum said she was feeling so much better today. So Mum and I were going to do something together today, and Granny was coming as well.

I put Jumper in her cage and carried her out to the car. Dad walked Mum out and told her to drive carefully. Then he gave me a kiss. Dad was driving into the office this morning and he was driving I hope he's not going to have a drink before work well he's a grown up and should know better.

We got to Granny's, and she wasn't ready. My granny's favourite saying before we go anywhere is, "Do you need a wee? Try and squeeze one out." Once Granny had gotten herself sorted, we were on our way. Still not much movement with Jumper. I was really sad, and Granny and Mum were saying she would be okay.

Granny sat in the car while Mum and I went into the vet's office. As soon as we got there, they called for Jumper to be seen. The vet was a lovely lady who gently got Jumper out of her cage. She was just lying on the table, and not moving much. The vet felt round by her ears and felt her tummy. "Oh", she said. "Jumper has a lump in her belly. How old is Jumper?" I told her she was eight years old. "That's a good age for a rabbit." The vet looked at me and said, "Lucy, I'm so sorry, but from what I can see and feel, it seems that Jumper has a tumour in her tummy. Unfortunately there's nothing we can do. She has had a good long life with you. I can give her an injection to put her to sleep now, or if you want, you can take her home and let her die with you. She's in no pain, and it won't be very long before she does die."

I started crying and couldn't stop. Mum asked what I wanted to do, and I said I wanted to take Jumper home with us. "Okay, that's what we shall do then."

The vet put Jumper into the cage, and we walked back to the car. Granny asked, "What's wrong, Lucy?"

"Jumper is dying. She's got a tumour in her tummy. I'm taking her home to die." Granny looked upset when I told her. I wondered, *Is this going to happen to my mum, Granny's daughter, Dad's wife?*

No one said anything on the way home. I was sat in the back, crying and watching Jumper's stomach go up and down. My head hurt because of all the tears I had cried. When we arrived home, Dad was still there. He must have seen us pull up as he came out and asked how it went. "Not good," Mum said.

"Dad, Jumper has a tumour in her tummy. We have brought her home to die."

"That's nice," he said.

"What do you mean, that's nice? Jumper is going to die."

"Come on. Let's go inside and talk about it. I shall tell you what I mean." We walked into the kitchen, and Dad put the kettle on. "Lucy, I meant that she won't die alone. She will have you by her side, and we can make it special when she has died. Unfortunately we all—animals, plants, and humans—have to die. We have talked about it."

Mum went upstairs and came down with a white cardboard box. "Lucy, why don't you decorate this box for Jumper for when she dies. Remember, we said anything in a box is a gift, so make it as pretty as you can. Write a letter, put some photos in there. Write on it, colour it, or just leave it the way it is. It's your choice. And when the time comes, Dad will dig a hole in the garden, and we can place her in there. You watch and wait for the beautiful flowers to grow and the butterflies to appear. And that is your thank-you from Jumper in return for you loving her. They say that butterflies are kisses from loved ones."

"But what about the winter? There are no flowers, and there is no butterflies. What then?"

"The frost and snow will come, and then little robins will appear. They say robins appear when angels are near."

"Okay, that's what I shall do. I will make it really special." I got all my pens and paints and started to colour my box. I kept going back and checking on Jumper but no change. On Jumper's gift box I painted a rainbow in all the colours, a bright sunshine, flowers, and butterflies. Then I painted a snowman and snowflakes, and then a little robin on a Christmas tree. I kept crying while doing this, and the paint was smudging. Mum, Dad, and Granny sat outside. They left me to get on with what I was doing but kept asking if I was okay. What can you say? "No, my mum's got cancer, and now my rabbit is dying with a tumour, so no, I'm not all right."

Today was so hot the big glass doors were open, and there was no breeze. It was nearly 4 p.m., I was still trying to find the right words to place in the box for Jumper. I was getting cross with myself because nothing was sounding right. Granny came into the kitchen, and I showed her Jumper's gift box. Then she said, "Lucy, I'm sorry that Jumper has passed away."

"No", I screamed. "She can't have. I haven't said goodbye. I haven't said goodbye." Mum and Dad came in. I have never cried so much. It felt like I hurt myself with a pain. No more Jumper. *What am I going to do now?*

Dad said, "I shall dig a hole. Lucy, where do you want Jumper to go. I picked a place that I could see from my bedroom window. Then Mum untied the scarf she was wearing around her head. She wrapped Jumper in it, and carefully placed Jumper in the pretty box I had decorated for her. I didn't notice Mum's head, but Granny did. I think it was the first time she had seen Mum with hardly any hair and was taken aback by it all.

Dad finished digging the hole and placed Jumper into the hole. Then he started filling the hole. In the end, we all were crying for one reason or another. After all these tears I had a headache and felt sick. Then Granny heard the ice-cream van and asked, "Do you want an ice cream, Lucy? That will make you feel better." It was more likely Granny wanted one. "Okay, then I will have one." Only Granny and I had an ice cream, and to be honest, it was really nice. Mum and Dad asked if I wanted to do anything, and I said no. They asked if I wanted to go and see Kate. I said no, that I just wanted to stay at home. Thinking about it, I hadn't heard from Kate, and I wasn't going to message her, especially after what happened at her house with her mum.

"Mum, can I ask you something?"

"Of course, Lucy."

"If your treatment doesn't work, will you want to die at home?"

"It depends how ill I become. But hopefully it won't come to that."

"Mum."

"Yes, Lucy."

"Can we shave the rest of your hair off?"

"Why not?" said Mum. It's falling out anyway, so let's do it."

Dad got the hair clippers out, Mum put the radio on, and that day turned out from being a sad one to a very memorable day and night.

The rest of the week and weekend were pretty normal if there is a normal. On Tuesday, Mum was back to the hospital for her another round of chemotherapy. Her hair was starting to grow, and her head was all fluffy, just like a baby's head. I still got upset when I thought about Jumper. I can't understand how one day she was here, and within a few hours, she had died. I know we all have to die but for everything in your body to just stop and not work anymore, it's a bit crazy. Each morning I looked out the window and still no flowers, still no butterflies.

I can't understand because I loved Jumper so much. Or is it because at the end I didn't look after her properly and didn't realise she was ill, and this is my punishment?

I was back at Granny's house. There were two weeks left before I start at the big school I was looking forward to a new school and meeting some new friends. Granny's playing bingo on her laptop. "Any luck, Granny?"

"No, not yet. Maybe you will be me luck, lucky Lucy."

"What are we going to do today, Granny?"

"Nothing, I'm afraid."

"Okay then. I glad I've got my phone for the internet." I looked at the clock, and it was 9.50. A great long day.

Granny said, "Lucy, come on. You can help me with jobs to be done without paying."

"What are we doing?"

"I'm sorting out my wardrobes."

"That's going to take weeks."

"You are so funny, Lucy." So off we went upstairs, and the next thing we knew, Mum and Dad were coming through the door, and it's just after 2.30. *Great! I can go home now.* But no, Mum and Dad wanted a cup of tea. Mum was saying that she has to have a scan as she is halfway through her treatment, and they are trying to arrange it so Mum and Dad can both take me to school on my first day. Mum still has to take loads of tablets every day, so fingers crossed that will be it, and our lives will be back to normal. After mum had finished talking about her upcoming tests, she said, "I've got a surprise for you, Lucy."

"Have you brought me a new rabbit?"

"No, Lucy, I haven't. But I have booked us all to go on a small trip to the coast, and we are staying in a caravan."

"How exciting," Granny said.

"Lucy, what do you think about that?" Mum asked.

"Yes, it will be fun. When are we going?"

"Tomorrow. So we have to get packed and sorted."

"Come on then, let's go!" I replied.

As soon as I got home, I ran upstairs and went straight to my wardrobe. I've got hardly anything to wear, but hopefully the weather will be really hot and sunny, so just shorts and T-shirts should do. I put all the clothes I wanted to take on my bed and went back downstairs. Mum was giving Dad a shopping list, so we didn't have to get things in the morning. I was really looking forward to this little holiday, going to the beach every day and fish and chips. And Dad said he's going to take me sea fishing. We haven't done that, so that's something new. Dad went shopping and had to pick up Granny on the way back as she was staying at our house so we could leave early in the morning. Mum and I were upstairs packing, and she said that she couldn't find half of her make-up. "Have you seen it, Lucy?

"No", I lied, but it was in my bedroom, under my bed. I would put it back later."

"Hello." It was Dad and Granny. "We've got the shopping. Does anyone want a cup of tea?" Granny asked. We were having a takeout tonight, then showers, and an early night. I went to bed about 8.30, normal time for me, but I knew I wouldn't be able to sleep. Dad said we are leaving at five o'clock tomorrow morning. I bet we don't 'cause Granny will have to go to the toilet a hundred before we get in the car.

At 5.30, we were still at home. Mum was sick this morning of all mornings. When mum was sick, she had brought back up her anti-sickness medication, so we had to wait a little longer. But at 6.15 a.m., we are on our way. We planned to stop when we are halfway there to get something to eat. Mum was in the back with me, sleeping. I just looked out the window thinking about how next Tuesday I would be going to a new school. We were going to be in the caravan till Saturday. That was three nights away from home. I was sure it was more than what Kate had ever done. And I still hadn't heard from her. At eleven o'clock, we stopped for something to eat. Granny was starving, which was nothing new. We ordered breakfasts and teas. The food came out really quickly, so we were in and out and back on the road within thirty minutes. We only had another hour to go, and we would be there.

Me and Granny sat in the car while Mum and Dad got the keys for the caravan. It looked nice here and really busy. Mum and Dad came out of the office with keys and a map of the site, as well as a list of things to do in the area. Our caravan was right beside the lake, and the patio doors opened out toward the lake. We all had our own rooms. I had my own bathroom, until I opened a door in the bathroom, and it went straight into Granny's bedroom. Mum and Granny wanted to unpack, and me and dad were going to explore the site. Dad brought everything in from the car and off we went. Dad got a call on his mobile. It was Mum saying to come back. They had finished unpacking, and we should all do something together.

When we got back, I told Granny and Mum all about the place, what we could do, and about the swimming pool and clubhouse. Mum suggested that we go to the harbour to see about a fishing trip for me and dad, and maybe get something to eat and an ice cream. Granny thought that was a great idea. The harbour was a twenty-minute drive, but it didn't seem that long. We found a parking space straight away, so off we were. Down at the harbour were lots of fishing boats doing different deals and trips. Dad said that it wouldn't be fair doing a whole day. Rather, it would be best to go for only a few hours, just in case I was seasick more like Dad. We chose a trip that started at 7 a.m. and finished at 12.30. We would be picked up and dropped off, so Dad didn't have to worry about parking or the car.

After that was booked, we walked down towards the beach. It was pure sand and no pebbles. Granny asked, "Do you want a bucket and spade?"

"No thank you, Granny." We sat on the beach for about an hour and then went to get something to eat. We sat outside a pub just watching the world go by. Dad got a menu and ordered some drinks. I got a lemonade and sat there thinking, *My mum has cancer, my rabbit has just died, I'm going to secondary school, and nobody here knows this. I wonder what things are going on in the life of someone 11 years old who lives down here.* Dinner came, and it was disgusting. But I was really too excited because I wanted to go to the arcades. Mum said, "If we go back to the caravan, then Lucy, you can go to the arcades. Is that okay with you, Lucy?"

"Yes, Mum." We got back to the car and headed back. When we got back to the caravan, Mum couldn't wait to get her shoes off. "I'm worn out now. Do you want a cup of tea?"

"No thank you. Granny can you take me to the arcades, please?"

"Of course. Can you give me five minutes?" That means half an hour. When Granny was ready, we walked towards the arcades I had £5.00, and I changed it all into 2ps. Granny said, "Once you have spent that, we shall walk back as you have a busy day tomorrow."

Me and Granny slowly walked back. When we got to the caravan. Dad and Mum were sitting outside, just looking at the fishing lake. It was so quiet, but these fly things kept biting me and making me itch. This caravan was so hot. All the rooms were small, but if you opened the windows, then flies came in.

Dad came in and woke me at 6.15 a.m. We were being picked up at 6.30am at the gates. Dad packed a bag with hats, sun lotion, drinks, and snacks. We walked up to the gates, and the man was waiting for us. When we got to the harbour, the boat was ready for us. There were six other people on the boat, but I was the only girl. The boat started, and the engines smelt disgusting of oil, and they were very noisy. Once we were out a few miles one of the boat workers gave us all a fishing rod with dead fish on it and showed us how to cast. Then shortly after that, we were all given a bacon sandwich. Dad was the first one to catch a fish, and the way he tried to reel in that fish, you would have thought it was a great white shark. But when he got it close, it was a herring. We all laughed fish. Dad was the only one who caught a fish on that trip. Never mind, it was good. When we got to the docks and said goodbye to everyone, we were taken back to our site. Dad walked slowly, and I was skipping. "Thanks, Dad. I really enjoyed that. It was fun."

When we got back to the caravan, Mum and Granny weren't in. Dad didn't have a key or his mobile on him. So Dad said, "Lucy, you will have to climb through the window." He helped me climb through the window, and I opened the door.

When Dad walked in, there was a washing-up bowl full of toilet paper covered in blood. No note, nothing. Dad rang Mum on her mobile, and it went straight to voicemail. Then he rang Granny's mobile, and she answered. "What's going on?" Dad asked Granny.

"Maria had a nosebleed, and it wouldn't stop. So I rang 999 and explained to them about her cancer. They said just to be on the safe side to bring her in, and we couldn't get hold of you."

"What's happening now?"

"They have done a blood test and are going to do an MRI scan only because she was getting one done next week."

"So where is she now?"

"Having her scan."

"Okay. I will stay here for a while because she's in the right place. I'm going to take Lucy swimming. Once we have been swimming, I will ring to see if there has been anymore news."

"Okay then."

Me and dad went swimming. He said there was nothing to worry about as Mum was in the right place, and there was nothing we could do. We didn't stay in the swimming pool for long because it was so busy, and obviously because of Mum. I think Dad was glad when I said, "Shall we get out?" Besides, my face was burning and bright red because Dad had not reminded me to put sun lotion on.

As we headed back to the caravan, Dad rang Granny. She said that Mum needs another blood transfusion, and the results were back from her scan. They were being emailed to her consultant. "They have asked if you could come and have a chat with the doctor at the hospital here," Granny added.

"No problem. We'll be in about half an hour." So off we went again on another hospital trip and waiting for Mum. This cancer was so inconvenient and rules our whole family's lives. I hated it.

When we arrived at the hospital, Granny was waiting at the main reception to meet us. Granny told Dad were to go, and Granny and I got something to eat. Granny and I were in the hospital restaurant when Dad came and found us. He told us that mum would be staying in tonight because of the blood transfusion, and unfortunately, we had to make our way home tomorrow because mum has to see her consultant. Great. That's so unfair. Just when we were doing something normal, this goes and happens. It's just not fair. Dad said, "I know, Lucy, that your mum feels absolutely sad that she has ruined the holiday."

"Well she has—again. She has ruined the plans as always."

"Lucy, that is so unfair of you. It's not your mum's fault she got cancer and is sick."

"Can I go and see her?"

"No, sorry. She's sleeping."

"What time are we leaving tomorrow? Five o'clock again?"

"No, about seven. We pick Mum up and drive straight home. I'll drop you and Granny off, and then Mum and I will go straight to the hospital to see the consultant. But tonight we can go to the clubhouse and see what's going on in there if you want."

"Okay then. But we will have to go back and pack before we can go out later," Granny said.

When we got back, I started packing straight away. Granny looked through the cupboards to see what to make for dinner. She decided on spaghetti, and then she started to pack. Once we finished packing, Dad put it straight into the car, so there would be less to do tomorrow. Granny prepared dinner while Dad was having a whiskey and sitting on the patio. "Dad, do you think it's bad news with Mum?"

"Lucy, I really don't know. Let's hope not."

"Dinner," Granny shouted. Dinner wasn't that bad. We ate outside, and it was pleasant. After dinner I had to do the dishes as the caravan had no dishwasher. I hadn't washed up for ages. Granny and Dad got ready, and I just couldn't be bothered. But I did brush my hair. We strolled along to the clubhouse and managed to find a table with some chairs. Me and Granny sat down, and Dad got the drinks. Granny had a wine; Dad had a whiskey and Coke. Granny commented, "You're drinking a lot."

"At the moment, I'm on holiday," Dad said. The entertainment was a mini disco for young kids and then after that bingo followed by a band. "Can I play bingo?"

"Of course you can, but only two books," Granny said. I had never played bingo before. Dad didn't play, just me and Granny. Dad was just getting drunk, and Granny was not impressed. There were four games of bingo, and we didn't win. But it didn't cost me anything. After the bingo we went back to the caravan. Tomorrow was going to be a long day.

Once back at the caravan, I rang Mum on her mobile. "Hello, Mum."

"Hello, Lucy. I'm so sorry that I have ruined everything for you. I'm so sorry."

"Mum, don't worry. It's not your fault you're poorly. Have you had your blood transfusion?"

"I'm having it now and all through the night."

"Mum, I love you."

"Lucy, I love you too. You are my world. Now go to sleep, and I will see you tomorrow."

"Okay, Mum. Night."

I woke up the next morning to the fire alarm going off because Granny was cooking bacon, sausages, eggs, and beans. It was just 6 a.m. And I wondered, *Who is doing the dishes? Me, of course, and I hadn't even asked for breakfast. But I supposed I should eat it.* Once we finished breakfast, yes I had to wash up. Dad put the dishes away, and Granny checked all the drawers and wardrobes. And trying to squeeze a wee out. Everything done, the car loaded, and we were on our way to get Mum. Dad parked right outside the hospital and went to reception. They brought Mum down. Once she was in the car, away we went. Mum looked yellow, old, and very fragile. How could she have changed overnight? We all were shocked at how Mum looked. It only took three hours to get home. Granny and I were dropped off first, and then Mum and Dad were on their way.

Granny said, "Well, Lucy, they have left us to unpack. Do you want a cup of tea?"

"Yes, please. Granny, do you think mum looked really poorly when we picked her up?"

"Yes I did, but let's not think the worst."

"Granny, Granny. Look! There are flowers where Jumper is buried." I opened the glass doors and went outside. While I was looking at the flowers, a butterfly came and sat on the flowers. It's true what Mum said, and I started to cry. But not sad tears; these were happy ones. Seeing this made me happy, very happy.

Me and Granny were clock-watching, waiting for Mum and Dad to come home. When they arrived, it was nearly 9 p.m., and Mum was so tired. Mum and Dad sat on the sofa and told me and Granny to sit down as well. "I'm sorry to say it's not good news," Mum said, and she started to cry. Then I started, and Granny did as well.

Dad continued, "Mum's cancer hasn't shrunk or gotten any bigger. The treatment is basically doing nothing for her. It's just making her feel sicker. They said that they can control the pain but unfortunately, as they've said all along, it's incurable."

"How long does Maria have left," Granny asked.

"We don't know; we didn't ask," Dad answered.

"We just have to take each day as it comes and be thankful," said Granny.

I couldn't believe it. I would be growing up without a mum. Dad without a wife, and Granny without a daughter. Dad got the whiskey. Granny said, "I'll have one of them," and Mum said, "Me too."

I just sat crying on the sofa. "I'm going to bed." I said my goodnights and cried myself to sleep.

Granny stayed last night. I think they all got drunk because there were a few empty bottles this morning. Nobody felt like doing anything today. It was just a sad day. This was my last weekend of summer holidays, and then secondary school. Where I will be labelled the girl whose mum has cancer. Then it will be the girl whose mum died. The whole weekend went so slowly, and nobody was really talking about the situation. I couldn't wait for school just for a change of scenery and something new.

Monday came and went, and then it was Tuesday. I had to be at school at 10 a.m. and go to the school hall. Mum, Dad, and Granny all came to take me there, but thank God they stayed in the car. "Lucy, we shall pick you up at 3 p.m. Just look out for the car," Mum said. Then they all shouted together, "Okay, have a good day!"

Went into the school hall and saw Kate, which was good. I walked over to her and asked how she was doing. "Good, thanks. What about you, Lucy?"

"Yeah, I'm okay. I think we are in the same class, that's good." Our teacher was Miss Brown a butch-looking teacher with white hair and really fat. I didn't learn much today. The only thing I was taught today was how to smoke with Kate and her cool friends. But you know what? I really don't care about school or anything. To be honest, life was crap, and my mum is dying, so sod school.

9 781665 595667